BURIED TREASURE

Other Teenage Mutant Ninja Turtle books available in
Yearling Books:

Teenage Mutant Ninja Turtles
    (a novelization of the movie) by B. B. Hiller
Six-Guns and Shurikens by Dave Morris
Sky-High by Dave Morris
Red Herrings by Dave Morris

TEENAGE MUTANT NINJA TURTLES

BURIED TREASURE

D A V E   M O R R I S

Illustrated by Phil Jacobs

A YEARLING BOOK

Published by
Dell Publishing
a division of
Bantam Doubleday Dell Publishing Group, Inc.
666 Fifth Avenue
New York, New York 10103

This work was first published in Great Britain by Yearling Books,
Transworld Publishers Ltd.

ISBN: 0-440-40391-X

Printed in the United States of America

June 1990

10 9 8 7 6 5 4 3 2 1

OPM

HEROES IN A HALF SHELL

Fourteen years ago a group of four ordinary turtles that had dropped into the storm drains beneath New York were found by Splinter, a master of the skill of ninjutsu, the ancient Japanese art of stealth and espionage.

Then . . . a leakage of radioactive goo exposed Splinter and his pets to mutating chemicals. Splinter turned into a giant talking rat, while the turtles became the Teenage Mutant Ninja Turtles— his wacky, wisecracking, crime-fighting ninja pupils.

With their human friend, April O'Neil, ace reporter on the Channel 6 TV News, the Turtles fight for what's right and foil the nefarious schemes of the Shredder, Splinter's evil renegade student.

Meet Leonardo, the coolly efficient sword-swinging team leader. Meet Donatello, the expert when it comes to machines; his swishing quarterstaff lays out his foes like bowling pins. Meet Raphael, the prankster, whose wry humor sees the team through perilous situations while his twin daggers send enemies fleeing in panic. And meet Michaelangelo, who's a master of the flying kick and the karate punch and is prepared to use them on anyone who gets between him and a pizza!

"This is a great pad, April," said Michaelangelo. "I'll bet you have some radical parties."

April had just finished showing the Turtles around her apartment. She folded her arms and looked at Michaelangelo sternly. "Mike, I don't want you—and this goes for all of you—I don't want you throwing any wild parties while I'm away. Have you got that?" She still remembered the last time she had had the Turtles around. Their horseplay had left two designer lamps and a coffee table smashed, and her cat had been so frightened that it had stayed away from home for a week. This time it had cleared out as soon as it saw the Turtles coming.

Donatello was peering studiously at her hi-fi. "Say, April," he muttered, "do the speakers still have that hiss? I could fix it while you're away."

"Don't touch it!" exclaimed April. "Don, I appreciate the offer, and I'm sure you know all about electronics and can fix any number of different gadgets, but I'd just as soon get a regular repairman in, okay?"

Leonardo brought her bags into the hall. "Don't worry about a thing," he said. "We'll take good care of the place while you're away. Gee, it's a pleasure just to get out of the storm drains for a week and enjoy a little luxury."

"Sure, and think what you're getting by letting us crash here," said Raphael.

April raised one eyebrow. "A headache?"

"No, no: guaranteed security. No burglar's going to rip off your stuff while the Teenage Mutant Ninja Turtles are on the spot."

"Whew, you certainly packed enough gear," said Donatello, testing the weight of April's bags. "You'd better let us help you carry it down to the car."

"By the way, April," asked Michaelangelo as they took the elevator down, "where is it you're going?"

April beamed. "I've been invited to stay as the houseguest of Arthur Horrocks. He's a wealthy retired businessman who makes a lot of contributions to charity. I did a feature on him for TV a few years back. Obviously he liked what I had to say, and he's asked me along to the big Halloween party he throws every year."

"Has he got a big place, then?" asked Leonardo.

"Sure—a really great old mansion up the coast near Smugglers Bay."

"Bigger than your apartment?" said Michaelangelo. Being used to their cramped den in the storm drains under New York, the Turtles thought that anything bigger than a broom cupboard was luxurious.

April laughed. "Of *course* it's bigger than my apartment, Mike. It's got seventeen bedrooms, twelve bathrooms, a games room, conservatory, oak-paneled dining room . . . all that kind of thing, and it's set on sixty acres of grounds."

"Wow!" gasped Michaelangelo. Though he had no idea how big an acre was, sixty of them sounded like a lot.

"And he's having hundreds of guests to his party," April went on. "It's a costume party, and there'll be fireworks, a band, plenty of champagne, and caviar . . ."

"Caviar!" said Raphael, licking his lips with relish. "What is that, by the way? And can you get it on pizzas?"

"I don't think so," said April, chuckling. The elevator doors opened, and the Turtles bustled her things across the lobby and into the car. It was still before dawn, since April wanted to make an early start on her long drive up the coast, so there was no one around to see them. April's cat glowered at them from atop a garbage can on the other side of the road.

"You won't forget to feed Fritz, will

you? A saucer of milk and some chopped liver—he doesn't like pizza."

"No wonder he's so small and timid," said Raphael, glaring back at the cat.

"Aww, April," said Michaelangelo as she got into the car, "can't we come along too? That party sounds like our kind of scene."

"Absolutely, definitely, categorically and without a doubt NO!" said April. She revved the engine. "I know the kind of havoc you four would be bound to cause. You'd only get yourselves and me into trouble, and I'd like to stay on Mr. Horrocks's good side. See you in a week or so, guys!"

"Oh, darn!" said Michaelangelo as April's car sped away. "I meant to ask her for the number of the local home-delivery pizzeria."

◆

"Whee!" said Michaelangelo a few days later. "Look at this. I'm sitting in a whirlpool!"

Raphael looked in through the bathroom doorway. "It's called a Jacuzzi, dummy."

"Jack who?" called Donatello from the living room. "Is he a singer? What kind of music does he do?"

Raphael strolled through with his hands over his ears. It was no wonder Donatello had not heard him properly: The hi-fi was going full blast, blaring out Mozart's *Requiem* at a floor-shaking volume. "See," said Donatello, beaming proudly as he held up his screwdriver. "I've got rid of that hiss on the speakers."

Leonardo reached out from the sofa and turned the volume down. "If we play records that loud, it's the neighbors who'll be hissing—at us," he said. He leaned back and munched at a slice of pizza. "Let's try to keep out of trouble, guys."

Michaelangelo emerged from the bathroom with a towel wrapped around him. "Did someone say *Neighbors* is on?" he asked, turning off the hi-fi as he walked through. The remote control was on April's glass coffee table; he picked it up and clicked it at the TV. "I'd say we were in the lap of luxury, dudes."

"Enough to make Master Splinter turn green with envy," agreed Donatello.

"Turn green as in turn turtle?" Raphael said. "Nah, Master Splinter's not into luxury; he's a bare-necessities kind of guy."

"Just think," said Michaelangelo as he flicked between channels, "if we think *this* is luxury, imagine how April feels about where she's staying."

Leonardo nodded. "It sounded ace to

me, all right. Except April didn't mention a gym, so not quite perfect."

Donatello was looking in a road atlas. "Smugglers Bay. . . . Yes, here it is, about a hundred and fifty miles up the coast near Rhode Island. Do you think it was once used by real smugglers?"

"Sure," said Raphael.

Donatello was dubious. "How do you know that?"

"Well, if it'd been used by accountants, for instance, they'd have called it Bookkeepers Bay, wouldn't they?"

The telephone started ringing. The Turtles all glared at it.

"Should we get that?" suggested Michaelangelo.

"I don't know about that," said Leonardo. "No one's supposed to know we're here, right? So what do we do—pick it up and say, 'Sorry, April isn't here to take your call right now; this is her answering service, your friendly neighborhood Teen Turtles'?" The truth was that he couldn't be bothered to get up off the sofa and answer the phone.

"Oh, look," said Donatello after it had gone on ringing for another half minute. "You get it, Raph; you're nearest."

"Not me," said Raphael, who was slouched in an armchair leafing through his martial-arts magazine. "I've got telephobia; that means I have an aversion to telephones."

"Telephobia?" said Michaelangelo, chuckling. "Is that a fancy word for hopelessly lazy, Raph?" He just ducked the cushion that Raphael threw at him. It sailed on across the room and collided with a painted glass vase. The four Turtles were rooted to the spot in horrified fascination as they watched the vase teeter this way and that until finally, with an awful lurch, it toppled to the floor and broke into a hundred pieces.

"Whoops," said Raphael.

"Ulp!" said Michaelangelo.

As if to add a note of censure, April's cat Fritz strolled imperiously in; glanced at the still-ringing phone; favored the Turtles with a long, withering glare; and jumped up to dislodge the receiver.

"Hello?" said a voice from the phone. "Hello? Guys, are you there?"

"It's April!" Donatello snatched up the receiver. "April, it's you."

"Of course it's me, Don," she replied. "Everyone else knows I'm on vacation and thinks the apartment's empty, so who else would be calling you?"

"Uh, of course. Sure." Ignoring the cat's scornful shrug, he called the others over. "So how's it going, April? Having fun?"

"Better tell her about the vase," whispered Leonardo.

"Not till I've found the super-glue!"

hissed Raphael. He vanished off into the kitchen to rummage in a drawer.

Donatello swallowed a nervous gulp. "Uh, listen, April, I'm afraid there was an accident. A vase got broken."

"Tell her the cat knocked it over," Raphael suggested, a wicked grin lighting up his face for a moment.

But, to everyone's surprise, April said, "Never mind about vases. There's something a lot more important than that going on. You'd better get up here."

"Where?" said Donatello. "To Smugglers Bay?"

"Yeah, on the double," said April. "Something's come up, and it's really urgent."

"Ask her what it is, Don. Is it the Shredder?" said Leonardo.

"Okay, I heard," replied April before Donatello had a chance to relay the message. "No, I don't suppose the Shredder's involved this time, but it's still pretty serious. Look, I haven't got time to explain over the phone. Just haul shell up here as fast as you can, huh?"

"Okay, Fritz," Leonardo said, already running toward the door as April hung up, "looks like you've got the place to yourself for a couple of days."

Raphael was the last out. "See you, you snooty fleabag," he growled at the cat. "Don't sponge off the neighbors too shamelessly." As the cat gave him a sneering look, he added, ". . . Otherwise you might get too fat to fit through your cat door!"

The cat watched, biding its time as Raphael went out and closed the door behind him. Though seemingly sleek and unruffled, inwardly it was bristling with malicious glee. It knew which sleeping bag Raphael used. . . .

It was evening by the time the Turtles reached Smugglers Bay, having hitched a surreptitious ride up the coastal highway in the back of a truck. Once there, it had only taken them minutes to find the signpost indicating Arthur Horrocks's estate. They surveyed the grounds from the branch of a tree just outside the perimeter wall.

"Maybe he's a millionaire philanthropist," said Raphael, "but it doesn't look like he's keen on uninvited guests." He was looking at the barbed wire running along the top of the wall. The barking of guard dogs came from inside.

"We could just call up April from a phone booth, and she'd get him to let us in," suggested Donatello.

Leonardo laughed under his breath. "I'm surprised at you guys! What would Master Splinter say? Getting in by ourselves is a great test of our ninja training."

"Boy, Leo," groaned Michaelangelo, "you sure love to do things the hard way."

Leo was not listening. He studied the garden beyond the wall for a few seconds and then pointed to a small bush. "We'll swing across the wall from here," he said, tying a line of strong cord to the branch. "Aim to land in that bush. It'll cushion your fall and also make a good hiding place if any guards are nearby."

"We might fool guards," protested Raphael, "but what about the dogs?"

Donatello was getting fired up by Leonardo's enthusiasm. "I've got a little gadget here that might do the trick," he said. He held up a small box like a pocket bleeper. "It gives off a high-pitched whine that humans can't hear, but it'll drive the dogs wild. I can set it to go off a few seconds after we get into the grounds, see? If I leave it here in the tree, it'll draw all the dogs to this part of the wall while we're slipping away across the garden."

The bleeper worked as well as Donatello had said. No sooner had they swung across the wall and concealed themselves in the bushes than a furious cacophony of barking erupted from the direction of the house. They could see guards carrying flashlights coming from all parts of the grounds, being fairly dragged across the lawn by their dogs.

"Should've brought Fritz along," grunted Raphael. "He'd have made just as dandy a diversion."

As the dogs and guards charged past, Leonardo pointed toward the mansion, and they made their way noiselessly through the evening shadows.

"Watch the closed-circuit cameras," whispered Leonardo, ducking as he approached the house. Two cameras set on poles were rotating to and fro, routinely sweeping the grounds for signs of any intruder.

"Or rather, don't watch them," said Raphael.

"They're just scanning on auto," Michaelangelo pointed out after timing the camera sweeps. "Probably no one's even watching the screens."

"Better safe than sorry, Mike," whispered Donatello. "By the way, there's an infrared beam here. Step high as you get onto the patio."

Lights were blazing from most of the downstairs rooms. "I hope we're in time for dinner," muttered Michaelangelo as they peered through a chink in the lounge curtains. There was no sign of anyone.

"These French windows are bound to be wired," said Leonardo. "Don, can you bypass the alarm?"

Donatello nodded. "Easy, but it'll take a few minutes."

Leonardo smiled. "Well, Mike's keen to eat, and I suspect that everybody's off in the dining room right now. We'd better find a faster way in if our bro' isn't to starve, huh? Come on, Turtles." He took out a pair of climbing spikes and began to ascend the wall.

"Oh, me and my big mouth," groaned Michaelangelo. "It looks as if I've given Leo another excuse to play the slavedriver." Nonetheless, he and the others also fitted climbing spikes to their hands and followed Leonardo up to the roof.

They found him already clambering into the chimney. "Halloween's a bit early for Santa Claus," he joked, "but at least it's a fair bet that the chimney isn't wired in to the alarm system."

Donatello reached out an arm to stop him. "Wait, Leo! What if there's a fire in the grate? You'll be turtle soup."

"As in teen, green, and roasted!" agreed Michaelangelo, nodding vigorously.

"Too bad we don't have April's cat Fritz along," said Raphael sourly. "We could've sent him down first to check whether it was safe."

Leonardo just shrugged and dropped out of sight. "I noticed there wasn't a fire when we peeked inside a moment ago," his voice came echoing up the chimney. "Don't you guys give me credit for any sense?"

Less than a minute later they were all standing on the hearth rug in the lounge—covered in soot. The other three glared at Leonardo. "NO!" they growled in unison.

At that moment, the lounge doors opened, and April walked in. She was about to refill her sherry glass, then did a double take as she saw the Turtles. "Hey," she said, "that was quick. I didn't expect you much before midnight. How did you like the ride in the limo?"

"Limo?" said Raphael with a side-long glance at Leonardo.

"After I told Mr. Horrocks about you—and don't worry, he can be trusted to keep a secret—he sent a chauffeured limousine down to the Big Apple to collect you. Air-conditioning, tinted windows, fridge stocked with chocolate bars, that kind of thing. I rang you back to tell you about it, but I couldn't get any reply."

"That's 'cause we were already on our way here," griped Donatello.

"Yeah," said Michaelangelo. "We hitched in the back of a garbage truck, came cross-country over a couple of meadows, climbed a tree, jumped over a wall, scrambled through a hedge, dodged a pack of mad dogs, clambered up onto the roof, and squeezed down the chimney."

April paused with her glass halfway to her lips and regarded them with a baffled expression. "Why? What did you do that for?"

Leonardo grinned weakly. "It was my idea, April. I thought it would help with our training."

"We learned one valuable lesson, all right, Leo," said Raphael. "We'll know not to listen to your bright ideas in the future!"

Before Leonardo could think of a reply, someone else came into the room. He was tall and thick-set, bald as a bean, with a Cuban cigar the size of a banana in his hand. "Mr. Horrocks," said April, "I'd like to present my friends, Leonardo, Donatello, Raphael, and Michaelangelo. If anyone can find the missing acorns, it's them."

"Well!" said Arthur Horrocks, puffing great clouds of blue smoke from his cigar as he stared in open astonishment. "Ms. O'Neil told me you were mutants and all, fellas, but I still wasn't quite expecting . . . well, you know . . ."

"Turtles?" supplied Michaelangelo.

Raphael twirled a sai deftly on the end of one finger. "Hey, you know what they say: Don't judge a book by its cover."

"Yeah," said Donatello. "We're hardbacks."

Mr. Horrocks laughed. "Okay, okay. I never judge someone by the color of his skin, anyway—not even if it's green! Ms. O'Neil says you're the best at what you do, and her opinion's good enough for me. So, can you get my acorns back?"

"Hold on just a second," said Leonardo. He led April to one side for a moment and whispered, "Did he just say *acorns*? Is this a gag, April—you brought us all the way up the coast to find a missing bag of nuts?"

"Perhaps I'd better explain," said Mr. Horrocks. He crossed over to the hearth, where a Van Gogh painting hung over the mantelpiece. He swung this out on a hinge to reveal a safe set into the wall. "I usually keep papers to do with my business in here, but sometimes cash and other valuables also." He punched in the combination on the safe's electronic lock and opened it. There was nothing inside.

"Looks like the cupboard is bare," said Raphael drily.

"It wasn't yesterday evening," put in April. "Mr. Horrocks opened it then to show me some special jewels he had just bought from an international dealer. At some time during the night somebody got in here despite all the guards and sophisticated alarms."

"That had to be some red-hot burglar. Even we would have had trouble," said Leonardo. Although outraged by the theft, he still had a tone of professional admiration in his voice.

Mr. Horrocks grunted. "To think of all the money this top-notch security

costs me, as well. Anyway, the thief broke into my safe and got clean away with the contents, including ten golden Fabergé acorns, together worth almost a million dollars!"

A few hours later the Turtles were already scouring the grounds for signs of how the burglar had got in and out. Mr. Horrocks had ordered the guards and their dogs inside for the night, April having assured him that Leonardo and the others would be more than adequate replacements if anyone else tried to break in. More importantly she impressed on him that they should keep the Turtles' involvement a secret, just in case one of the guards was in league with the burglar.

"Whoever it was would have to have been really nimble to get in the same way we did," said Michaelangelo, looking at the branch of the tree they had swung from.

"A regular cat burglar," agreed Donatello.

"Great," said Raphael. "Let's just arrest Fritz and be done with it."

Leonardo was examining the lawn and flower beds for any trace of footprints. "Raph, what've you got against that poor cat?"

"Poor cat?" blustered Raphael. "That animal's no better than a beggar with a tail, a regular feline freeloader. Why, I—hey, guys, look at this!"

They hurried over to find Raphael

crouched over a patch of soil at the border of a flower bed. "That is strange," said Donatello, nodding. "The rest of the garden looks so well tended. It's unlikely the gardener would have left a patch of turf dug up like that."

"It looks like something's been buried there," said Michaelangelo.

"Let's see . . ." Raphael dug his fingers into the soft soil and poked around. After a moment he touched something small and hard. He pulled it out of the hole and wiped the mud from it. There was a yellow glint in the moonlight.

"Gold!" said Leonardo with a gasp.

"It's one of the acorns, all right," said Raphael. He spat on the muddy object and used his wristband to clean it until it sparkled like new.

The Turtles looked at one another blankly. They were all thinking the same thing: Why go to all the trouble of stealing the gold acorns and then leave one of them buried in the garden? And if the thief had buried this one, had he done the same with the others?

Michaelangelo looked around the Horrocks estate with a sinking heart. Now he knew how big sixty acres was. The prospect of going over the whole place looking for the other nine acorns was daunting, to say the very least. "Better get out the fine-tooth combs, dudes," he said.

"Not just yet," said Leonardo. "I think we'd better get this one back to Mr. Horrocks first. Then we'll get some sleep and continue the investigation tomorrow. This really is turning out to be a mystery that'd baffle Sherlock Holmes."

❖

April called on them early the next morning. They had been given a suite of rooms in one wing of the Horrocks mansion, and the latticed windows gave a commanding view of the grounds. Leonardo was standing there looking out over the trees that blazed like red gold in the pale autumn sunlight.

"Hey, April," said Michaelangelo, yawning as he lay back on a huge four-poster bed. "This room alone is bigger than your whole apartment."

"Don't rub it in, Mike," she said. "Now, how do you guys feel about a working breakfast?"

She turned and gestured, and Mr. Horrocks's butler wheeled in a trolley laden with silver trays. A succulent smell wafted into the room along with him. Immediately the Turtles rushed over to the breakfast table, licking their lips as they watched the butler smoothly lift the covers to reveal eggs, bacon, smoked fish, toast, home fries, and tomatoes.

"I'll bet this is the first time you've fed a quartet of hungry mutant turtles," chuckled April to the butler as the four fell to demolishing their breakfast.

"It is, as far as I can recall, miss," replied the butler unflappably. He set a coffeepot down on the table. "Will that be all?"

"I think it'll do for now," said April. "Thanks, Smithers. I'll give you a call if they look in imminent danger of starving."

"Very good, miss." Smithers retreated inaudibly from the room and closed the door with a modest click. He could have taught even the best ninja something about moving silently.

For a few moments it was sheer pandemonium around the table as the Turtles squabbled over the silverware, wrestled for the salt and the ketchup, and fell over one another for second helpings. After a while, with their appetites satisfied, April was able to call them to order.

"Oooh, I think I've eaten too fast," groaned Michaelangelo, suppressing a burp.

"Or too much," said Raphael. He yawned and looked out of the window. "It's only just dawn! This is a bit pig's tail, isn't it?"

"Pig's tail?" said April.

"Yeah, pig's tail: twirly. 'Twirly' as in 'too early'—get it? Maybe I'll just go back to bed for half an hour . . ."

Leonardo threw a rolled-up napkin at him. "And you're being a bit sloth's eyelids, Raphael—by which I mean lazy as in *lazy*! Have you forgotten we have a job to do?"

Raphael caught the napkin and looked at it, still yawning.

"It's a napkin, Raph," said April with a laugh. "But, knowing you guys' table manners, you wouldn't recognize one if it hit you on the head. All the same you don't have as big a job ahead of you as you thought. Mr. Horrocks has called in some people with metal detectors. They're already out scouring the grounds for the other missing acorns."

"So I can take a nap after all?" said Raphael.

"No," said Leonardo.

"Why not?"

"Because you're taking an ice-cold shower instead," chortled Donatello. "Get him, guys!"

◆

An hour later they gathered in Mr. Horrocks's study downstairs. Horrocks sat behind his desk, looking askance at an unlit cigar he was rolling between his hands. He usually smoked when he was trying to solve a particularly knotty problem, but problems didn't usually come up so early in the day. He really did not feel like a cigar at the moment. "It just doesn't make much sense to me," he said. "The people I got in with those metal detectors have turned up all nine of the remaining acorns. They were buried at random points around the estate. Why go to all that bother and then leave the loot behind?"

"Maybe the thief intended to collect it later," suggested Leonardo.

Horrocks snorted and lit his cigar after all. "Hardly a lot to carry, was it? You could fit all ten of them inside a paper bag."

"And the other weird thing is that they were buried all over the estate," said April. "Even if there was some reason to bury them, why not leave them all in one spot?"

Donatello looked pleased with himself. He had had an idea. "Do you know what Sherlock Holmes used to say? He said that when you rule out what's impossible, whatever remains—however incredible—has got to be the answer."

"Didn't he also say, 'A lemon tree, my dear Watson'?" said Raphael sarcastically.

"Wait a minute," said Leonardo. "What's your idea, Don?"

"Well, it seems to me that if the thief—or thieves (there might have been more than one, of course, but let's say it was one for the sake of argument)—if he'd wanted the gold acorns, then he wouldn't have left them behind. What that means is, *there must have been something else in the safe*. That's what he was really after."

"There were just some papers," said Mr. Horrocks. "Nothing top secret or anything worth money to anyone. Sometimes I keep business documents and plans in the safe, but there wasn't even anything like that this time."

"What sort of papers were they, Mr. Horrocks?" said Leonardo. Donatello's logic had convinced him at least.

"A sheaf of old documents that've been in the safe for years. I think there was a plan of the house from when it was first built a couple of hundred years ago. I'd hardly glanced at it. I suppose it might've been worth something as an antique—maybe a couple of hundred dollars to a collector, but nothing like the million dollars in gold that was left behind."

"So that's what the thief was after," murmured Donatello, half to himself.

Michaelangelo was sitting in a leather armchair juggling a couple of onyx paperweights. "That's a lot of trouble for something worth only two hundred dollars, Don," he said without taking his eyes off the paperweights.

Donatello strode over and snatched them out of midair. "Yes, but don't you see . . . ? The plan must have shown something that you wouldn't find on a modern map of the house. Something only the original owners knew about—"

"Secret passages!" yelled Michael-angelo.

Donatello took a bow. "What else? QED!"

"What does *QED* stand for?" asked Raphael.

" 'Quite Excellent, Donatello,' of course," said Donatello. "We figured there were originally smugglers in this part of the country, right? Well, think what an advantage it'd be to a band of smugglers to have hidden tunnels connecting a house like this to some point down by the sea—say a sheltered cove where they could drop off their booty, then bring it up to the house right under the noses of the revenue patrols."

"And you think those tunnels are still there?" asked April.

"Why not? And if they were shown on the plan, that means whoever stole it now knows a secret route straight into the house."

The others needed no more convincing. They immediately set about trying to find any secret panels that might conceal the tunnels Donatello suggested. For four skilled ninja, it did not take very long. They only had to look in the places where they, as experts in stealth and security, would have put such tunnels. Within half an hour they had found three in the east wing alone.

"They go right down to the beach, all right," announced Raphael, emerging with a flashlight after a foray along one of the tunnels. "There's a kind of concealed bay where the smugglers must have brought their ships for unloading."

Mr. Horrocks flicked ash from his cigar. "I'm still in the dark," he rumbled. "I mean, whoever stole the plans got into the house once without being spotted—what did they need the location of the tunnels for?"

"Tomorrow evening you're giving your big Halloween party, right?" explained Leonardo. "I should think there'll be quite a few VIPs along."

"That's an understatement, if ever I heard one," said Mr. Horrocks. "Why, there'll be politicians, top scientists, media figures, important industrialists. . . . You name them, they'll be here. I've got over a hundred guests coming; the annual Horrocks Halloween party is the talk of high society."

"Rich people?"

"Sure, they're rich. Most of the people I know are."

"Rich pickings for kidnappers, then," said Leonardo. "My guess is that they sent one guy in to filch the plans but that they'll come in force through the tunnels tomorrow night. They probably intend to overpower your security men and make off with one or more of the guests."

"Humph!" said Horrocks. He stubbed out his cigar angrily and reached for the phone. "Wait till I make a few calls. I'll have those tunnels bricked up and then we'll arrange a security team to arrest these kidnappers if they show up."

Leonardo put his hand on the phone. "Wait. For the ransom they could get for a couple of your VIP guests, we're not talking about any ordinary gang of criminals. They could be international terrorists, quite possibly armed with automatic weapons. Your security men could get hurt—or worse—and there's always the risk that some of the gang would get away."

"Okay, son, I'm listening." Horrocks folded his arms and sat back. "You've got a better plan?"

"Just let us handle it. We'll allow the kidnappers to get inside the house, then block off the tunnels so they don't have an escape route. With our training I'm pretty sure we can round them up quietly and without fuss."

"As an additional security measure, restrict the party to upstairs rooms," suggested Donatello. "Since the tunnels all come out on the ground floor, we'll be able to intercept the kidnappers before they even get close to endangering any guests."

Horrocks was dubious. "You're suggesting I go ahead with the party? Isn't that a bit dangerous? Someone might get caught in the crossfire."

"Quite a few of your guests must be on their way already," said Raphael. "And we need the party to go ahead as planned in order to lure the kidnappers out of the woodwork, so to speak. But no one at the party need know a thing. Why alarm them unnecessarily?"

"I don't know . . ." said Horrocks, chewing his lip. "You only need to miss one. If he gets upstairs with a submachine gun under his arm, why, people might get hurt! Ever heard of reckless endangerment? I'd be in court for years!"

A sudden inspiration made Michaelangelo perk up. "One of us will be at the party in person, to run a last line of defense," he said. "Since it's in costume, I can mingle right in among the guests and nobody will notice; they'll just think I'm decked out for trick or treat. If one of the kidnappers gets past the others downstairs, I'll stop him."

"Who said it'd be you?" said Raphael, winking at the others.

"Hey, dudes," said Michaelangelo, "I never miss a party!"

Guests started to arrive for the party around noon the following day. By early evening more than a hundred people were gathered in the upstairs gallery of the house. Among the profusion of Halloween costumes—giant rabbits and gorilla suits as well as the traditional spooks, witches, and goblins—nobody paid any particular attention to Michaelangelo. One man, apparently an admiral from the Pentagon, had already drunkenly mistaken him for a Japanese diplomat whom he knew. Master Splinter had told Michaelangelo enough about the Japanese countryside for him to go along with the misunderstanding. Such a deception was useful in fact; it allowed him to mingle with the guests without arousing anyone's suspicion. He helped himself to another hors d'oeuvre and listened politely while the admiral told him about U.S. naval doctrine.

Outside, the other three had settled themselves in a vantage point under the eaves of the house. There they crouched, absolutely motionless, staring out through the thickening shadows of nightfall. Anyone looking up would have thought they were just a trio of rather odd gargoyles—or perhaps Styrofoam decorations in keeping with the party's Halloween theme.

By eight o'clock all the guests had arrived. From inside the house they could hear the muffled pounding of music and the hubbub of merry conversation. A cold northerly wind started to blow.

"I expect Mike's having a nice time," grumbled Raphael after another hour had passed.

Half an hour went by. "Yep," said Donatello through chattering teeth.

"Shush!" hissed Leonardo fifteen minutes later. "Scope out the far corner of the garden, guys."

It was just possible to make out a dark shape detaching itself from the deeper darkness under a tree and slipping closer to the house. Behind it another shadow came into sight and followed the same path, zigzagging from shrub to shrub.

"Ninja training, I'm almost sure of it," was Donatello's opinion.

Leonardo was still staring hard across the lawn. Two more shadowy figures glided into view momentarily and darted toward the house. They moved rapidly and with astounding agility, leaping obstacles such as flower beds as though weightless, occasionally freezing for a moment like statues as they seemed to listen for even the slightest sounds carried on the wind.

Leonardo switched to ninja sign language. "Too good for Foot Clan ninja," he signaled to the others with his fingers.

"M-much t-too good," signaled Raphael. His fingers were so cold that his sign language came across like stuttering.

"Do we take them?" said Donatello's fingers.

Leonardo nodded. "Yes, right about . . . NOW!"

The last word was delivered not in sign language but in a powerful martial shout that cracked out through the night like thunder. Hearing it, the four shadowy figures froze rigid and looked up. As they did so, the three Turtles launched themselves out from the eaves, swung off the branches of a nearby tree, and landed right in the midst of the intruders.

But the advantage of surprise did not last longer than a split second. Even before Leonardo had recovered his balance after the jump, he had to parry a yari-spear thrust from the nearest of the intruders. He ducked to one side and then the other, narrowly avoiding two further jabs of the spear executed in quick succession.

Donatello was attacked by two at once. He managed to use his bo-staff to pole-vault over their heads, but they spun around instantly and slashed at him with shortswords. He was forced to do a double backflip. That gave him some distance to deploy his staff against the shortswords, but it also carried him away from the thick of battle. One of the intruders followed up, brandishing his sword with circular feinting movements. "Nice bo technique," Donatello heard him mutter. "Iga Province—style of ninjutsu, if I'm not mistaken."

Raphael was attacked by the fourth intruder, who was armed with a pair of lethal nunchuk-sticks. He caught the first swing in the prongs of his sai and tugged the weapon out of his opponent's hand. Not discouraged, the intruder immediately followed through with a flying kick that Raphael was hard pressed to dodge.

The Turtles had still not managed

to get a good look at their assailants in the deep darkness under the tree. Leonardo had a remedy for that. He pulled a flare from his belt and dropped it to the ground, where it fizzed for a moment and then blazed alight. For a few seconds the area under the tree was lit almost as bright as day, and the two groups saw one another clearly for the first time.

"What on earth—?" gasped Leonardo.

He was not the only one to be astonished. For the four intruders, revealed in the light of the flare, were mutant squirrels clad in black kevlar combat jackets. They wore night goggles and had Uzi rifles slung across their backs, and each was armed with a close-combat weapon.

The flare died down to a soft glow, but still no one moved. "You're . . .

you're mutants too!" said one of the squirrels at last.

"Yeah, but we're the good guys, pal," said Raphael. He licked his lips warily and held up his sai-daggers. The squirrels seemed to have broken off their attack, but he had yet to be convinced that it was not a trick.

"We're the good guys also," protested one of the squirrels, the one with the spear. "I'm Wolfgang. This is Johann." He indicated the squirrel whom Raphael had disarmed, who was just now retrieving his nunchuk-sticks.

"And I'm Ludwig," chipped in one of the shortsword-users.

"Me, I'm Antonio," said the other. "We're the Mutant Squirrel Superspies."

"Shouldn't that be the 'Mutant Squirrel Kidnappers'?" said Raphael with a growl; he still refused to relax his guard.

"We aren't the kidnappers," said Wolfgang, "but I'm glad you've realized that they're on their way. It'll save us a lot of explaining. We're here to stop them, you see."

Leonardo folded his arms. "All right, supposing we accept that you and we are on the same side. How about explaining who you are? Like, how did you get to be mutants?"

"The same way you did, probably," said Ludwig. "Once we were ordinary squirrels, bright-eyed and bushy-tailed, but we got exposed to radioactive mutagen."

"That's not quite the same as us," said Raphael pedantically. "We were ordinary turtles, not squirrels."

"Naturally," continued Ludwig. "Well, fortunately we were adopted by a retired Mossad agent and trained in espionage techniques."

"Mossad," said Donatello. "They're

the Israeli secret service—probably the best spies in the world. That explains why you guys are as good as you are. But how come your names don't sound particularly Israeli?"

"Our mentor was a music buff," said Johann. "What about you fellows—considering you're ninja, you don't sound very Japanese."

"We're not; we're *American* turtles," said Leonardo. "I'm Leonardo, this is Donatello, and this is Raphael. Our fourth team member is covering the party—that's Michaelangelo."

"American. Uh-huh." Ludwig nodded, smiling. "Don't tell me, let me guess: you were taught by an Oriental master ninja, who named you after famous painters?"

"You got it," said Raphael. "But that's enough nonsense; how about letting us in on what's going down here tonight?"

Wolfgang turned serious. "Through our links with various spy networks, we got wind of a plot by international terrorists to kidnap Arthur Horrocks. We had to break into Horrocks's safe a couple of nights ago to get a complete plan of the house and grounds. We knew the criminals already had a copy."

"Why not just approach Horrocks and ask him to cooperate?" asked Donatello.

Wolfgang spread his hands. "Be real. Would you trust four mutant squirrels who just came swinging into your study one night? No, we thought it was better to do things undercover. Unfortunately when we cleaned out the contents of the safe, we didn't look at what we were taking. It was only later that we realized we'd accidentally stolen the golden acorns."

"Okay," said Raphael, "but why did you bury them around the grounds?"

"Old habits die hard," explained the squirrels with a shrug.

"Shall we get Mike?" asked Donatello as they crept into the darkened ground floor of the mansion.

Leonardo shook his head. "No, we'd better stick with the original plan. I'd like to know we have someone up there with the guests, just in case of trouble."

The music and chatter from the

party were much louder here inside the house. As they approached the stairs, Wolfgang leaped up onto the balustrade with remarkable agility. "We expect the kidnappers to show around midnight," he said. "It doesn't matter which of the tunnels they enter by. These stairs are the only way up."

Raphael reached into the utility pack on his belt and produced a handful of shuriken—slender iron spikes. Usually they were used for throwing, forcing an enemy to cover his face so that he was distracted from noticing another attack. This time, though, Raphael had another use in mind. "Once we're sure the kidnappers are inside, I'll use these shuriken to spike the hidden panels shut. That way we have them trapped."

"There's one thing that bothers me," murmured Antonio. It looked as though he was literally sniffing the air for danger. "What if any of the guests hear the commotion and get nosy? It wouldn't do to have them wander down into the middle of a fight."

"Don't worry," said Leonardo. "Humans don't have as sensitive hearing as you squirrels. They won't hear a peep over the noise of the party."

Johann was exploring the darkened corners of the hall. "I hope you're right," he said. Suddenly he stiffened like a wire brush. "Wait! Hear that, friends? Sounds like our terrorists are turning up a little early."

The Turtles had not heard anything, but they knew that the Squirrels' senses would be better than their own. Leonardo clicked his fingers as the signal to action, and everyone melted silently into the shadows.

They waited with bated breath. Thirty seconds passed, measured out excruciatingly by the grandfather clock in the hall, and then a door opened. A crack of light appeared, obviously cast by a flashlight. They could hear harsh voices lowered in whispered discussion. After a few seconds another door opened on the other side of the hall. A flashlight clicked on and off several times in rapid succession.

"Morse code," whispered Donatello. "They're signaling that the coast is clear."

"Yuk, yuk," chortled Raphael. "Boy, are they in for a surprise!"

The doors opened wider, and two groups of black-clad figures stepped into the hall. Spreading out along the walls, they made their way over to the stairs.

Raphael had a sudden inspiration. Grabbing a drape that hung down from the balcony overhead, he clambered silently up until he was level with the banister. Then, leaping across, he slid down like a skater and careened like a cannonball right into the midst of the kidnappers.

"Trick or treat!" he yelled as several of the kidnappers went flying. "Don't you bozos know that this party is strictly by invitation only?"

Leonardo and the others did not lose a second getting in on the action. As they darted foward, one of the flashlight beams illuminated them head-on. The shock of seeing themselves under attack from a bunch of animal-mutants unnerved the nearest kidnappers, who threw up their arms in astonishment.

"Giant turtles and giant squirrels!" gasped one. "I swear I'll never touch strong liquor again as long as I live."

"They're just short guys in Halloween suits, you dink!" snarled the leader. "Come on, pile in. There's only seven of them."

One of the kidnappers was leveling a pistol. Johann charged in toward him,

nunchuk swinging like a rotor, then half-turned at the last moment so that the kidnapper got a faceful of bushy tail. As he spluttered and tried to clear the hair out of his eyes, the nunchuk lashed out, catching him on the top of the head. He fell, stunned, and the gun went off wildly. Fortunately the bullet ricocheted harmlessly off a suit of antique armor that stood at the bottom of the stairs. The bullet itself missed everyone, but the impact loosened the armor's upraised arm so that it swung down and clouted another kidnapper on the back of the neck. He, too, fell in a dazed heap.

"Nice moves, dude," Leonardo called out as he knocked down a kidnapper with the flat of his sword.

"Don't use your guns, idiots!" shrieked the leader to his men. "You're most likely to hit one of your own team.

Show these freaks the karate I taught you."

"Karate!" cried Donatello happily. "That's our kind of rumble." He threw his quarterstaff like a javelin, and it hit a kidnapper right in the midriff. He went flying backward with his arms windmilling wildly and bowled over another two. They lay in a heap, groaning, as the leader raced forward and angrily launched a karate kick at Donatello's head. Donatello twisted around and leaned forward slightly so that the kick landed on the back of his shell. As his opponent's foot skidded across the shell, he turned and grabbed the outstretched leg and threw the man over his shoulder. He struck the marble floor of the hall with terrific impact and slumped unconscious.

"Aww, you cheated, Don," said Raphael as he punched his own opponent. "That was more like judo than karate."

Wolfgang was right between two assailants. As they rushed in to attack him, he jumped high into the air and grabbed their heads, knocking them together with a crack that made everybody wince.

"That's the last of 'em, I think," said Ludwig.

"Oh no, it wasn't!" said Raphael in a horrified tone. "Look." He pointed up the stairs, and they whirled to see a lone kidnapper racing off along the balcony toward the party.

"Yipe!" cried Leonardo. "If that guy panics and starts firing into the crowd, a lot of people are going to get hurt." He charged off up the stairs, closely followed by Donatello and Raphael. The Squirrels had a quicker way to ascend, nimbly scaling the drapes that Raphael had made use of earlier. Even so, they all knew that they could not catch the man before he reached the party. They felt sick with horror at the thought of what might happen. . . .

The man reached the door at the end of the balcony and fumbled at the handle. He already had his pistol in his hand and a wild look in his eyes. Suddenly the door shot open, and Michaelangelo came charging out. His hands were pressed over his mouth and he hardly seemed to notice the kidnapper, whom he slammed into with jarring force. The man shot back along the balcony just as Wolfgang reached the balustrade. Without pausing, he swung over onto the landing and dived behind the man's legs. As he toppled, Leonardo came up the stairs and gave him a karate-punch haymaker that laid him out cold.

Michaelangelo paid no attention at all, not even to the astonishing sight of four mutant squirrels, much less the pile of unconscious kidnappers in the hall below. He barged straight past everyone and into the bathroom.

April stepped out from the party and closed the door behind her. "Mike, are you okay—? Hey, what's going on h . . ." Her voice trailed off as she caught sight of Wolfgang and his brothers. She stood with her mouth gaping open.

"April, you look like a fish out of water," said Raphael.

She closed her mouth. "Uh, look, would anyone mind telling me what's going on here? Who *are* these guys?"

Wolfgang and the others bowed. "Dear lady," he said, "allow me to introduce myself and my brothers, who have been privileged to act as the Turtles' comrades-in-arms."

"Another bunch of mutants?" said April after she had heard the full explanation. "And squirrels this time? I think I must be going *nuts!*"

There were groans all around. Leonardo turned his attention to the kidnappers. "Once we've got these felons tied up and the police have been called, I don't see why we shouldn't all join the party."

Donatello nodded. "We certainly deserve it after a good night's work—even if I say so myself. And as Mike said, everyone will just think we're in costume."

"Omigosh," said April. "I forgot all about Mike. He was just piling up his plate from the snack table, then the next thing I knew he went charging out of the room."

"Good thing, too," said Raphael. "If he hadn't stopped that gunman, things could've got nasty."

April went over to the bathroom

door. "Mike," she called. "Mike, are you all right?"

They heard the lavatory flush. After a moment the door opened, and Michaelangelo came out with a sheepish expression on his face. "I'm fine," he said. "I just made the mistake of trying that caviar stuff—and, oh boy, it tasted so salty and yucky, I had to get to the bathroom right away and spit it out."

Raphael laughed and patted him on the back. "I'll buy you a dozen pizzas to take the taste away, Mike. I'm just glad that for once in your life you had the good manners to run to the bathroom!"